Shadows Through the Fog

Amanda Leanne

Published by Mune's Quill, 2017.

This is a work of fiction. Similarities to real people, places, or events are entirely coincidental.

SHADOWS THROUGH THE FOG

First edition. August 30, 2017.

Copyright © 2017 Amanda Leanne.

ISBN: 979-8215698266

Written by Amanda Leanne.

Table of Contents

Table of Contents 1
The Day I Danced with Death 6 5
Secret Medicine 8 7
Something's Changed 10 9
Dinner's at 7 14 15
Do You Part 22 27
The Other Side of the Mirror 26 33
Daryl Had an Idea 28 35
When the Chains Snap 34 45
Are you awake? 41 55
Under the Bright Lights 44 59
Couch Co-Op 52 71
The Little Lost Faery 56 77

Dedication

To those who suffer from their own inner demons, the dark thoughts and twisted shadows of the soul. To those who know depression and anxiety and insomnia like a familiar lover, forever tapping on your window. To those who know pain and know hurt and know emptiness. You are not alone.

I also dedicate this book to my son, Adeon, and the love of my life, Kris. Both have always been the moonlight that guides me through the dark, and for that, I am forever thankful. How I love you both, so much.

More from Amanda Leanne 57

AMANDA LEANNE

Introduction from the author:
I have always been a fan of the dark and macabre. From an early age I suffered from insomnia. My mother had the same affliction and often we both would end up sitting in the living room watching old horror movies on television or reading stories by Stephen King or Edgar Allen Poe. I didn't mind gore, but I was much more interested in the idea of situations that were terrifying or hopeless or even sad.

I suppose I was the weird person that preferred the movies that everyone died at the end or the bad guy won, because to me, that was more realistic. Life is an Olympic size swimming pool of disappointments, failures, sadness, and anger. Yes, I do have a bit of an issue with depression and being pessimistic, but I like to see it as "prepared for the worse." My motto was always to expect the worst case scenario, because the outcome was much more likely to be better than that and I would have the pleasure of being wonderfully surprised.

Some of these stories are gory and graphic, some are sad and melancholy, but most are pretty dark in one fashion or another. Consider this book my trail mix of dark and disturbing. I haven't decided what direction I want to take my fiction writing, so this is also a sort of talent show for me to help decide my winning direction. I want to see what people like, what gets to them, what hangs in their minds long after they have read my stories.

I know that no one will like all of the tales in this book, in fact you may not like half of them, but that's why I wanted to put so many in here in the first place! So if you do not care for one, move on to the next one. Some are short, some long, some gory, some sad, first person, third person, and so on. Some may seem really vague or confusing, and that's okay. I can be like that, sometimes. I did try to arrange the first few as to ease you into the depravity of my mind.

I do hope you like at least one, and if you do, please tell me which one and why you like it so much. I can't base my menu off of the favorites on the sample platter if no one tells me which ones they tasted.

I thank you, though, regardless, for endeavoring to read my book. Hopefully you can find something to enjoy within its pages.

Amanda Leanne

The Day I Danced with Death

I saw death today, but he didn't see me. I don't know how I knew it was death, just something in me felt the urge to go the other way, to turn and run, my mind felt frightened but my heart calmed as I wished that he would see me.

Momma always told me death looked however we wanted it to. If we wanted death to be kind and comforting, it came as a sweet and kindly grandmother. If we feared death and could not think our way around it, it came as something dark and sinister. If we wanted death, if we ached for death, then death would come as someone we had always wanted.

Death was my soul mate. His eyes were the eyes I always sought in a crowd. His hair was long and silky and begged my fingers to trail through the fine strands. His lips invited mine, begging me to taste the end of pain and awaken warmth I had never felt. He was tall and lithe, his arms strong and his shoulders wide and proud.

Death didn't see me, though. No matter what we want death to be, no matter what it comes to us as, we don't get to decide what death sees. Sickness, pain, innocence, evil, darkness, anything we are made of is what we will be. So I saw death, but he didn't see me.

Momma must have known I saw something; she stared at me and said I was smiling. I never smile, not anymore. As she walked around to grab the handles of my wheelchair, she tried to see what I saw. Her eyes narrowed as she scanned the crowd in front of us, but she didn't see death as I saw him.

As we left the park, I felt sad and empty. I had seen him, but how could I make him see me? I had invited him over, with razors and pills, but only in my dreams. I had written him love letters in my head as my eyes shed tears of pain. I had begged him to come to me, to hold my hand and kiss my cheek, but my pleading was always in vain.

When we were home and momma got me on the couch, I stared past the television and the glass panes of the window beyond. The sky was supposed to be blue, the clouds white, but to me it was shades of gray. The color was fading, it had been fading, and I was beginning to forget what the words even meant. What is red? Blue? What shades are warm and cold? The only color I knew was the one in Death's eyes, as he watched the people around him.

The days and nights bled together, the dark and light a ceaseless circle. The pain began to bring back a color, the white-hot reds of suffering. My skin felt red, my mouth was red, and my bones were turning the same shade as my blood. And though the days were worse, and my memory and thoughts were turning to sand, I still remembered seeing Death.

I think I cried, I do not know. I tried taking the medicine and drinking the soup. Soon the tubes were my support and the wheelchair was permanently parked, and still I thought of my soul mate. He was out there working, being an old woman, a shadow, a smiling child, and what people needed him to be. But he still had yet to see me.

Then the day came, where my eyes drifted through the foggy shades of my room, and something stood in front of me. I could see nothing clearly, except for him, and finally, he could see me. He held out his hand, reaching for mine, and happily I gave it. I rose from the bed as he twirled me around, and into his arms I went.

He saw me, and I saw him, my prince, and my defeater of pain. He loved me and I loved him, and together we danced my life away.

Secret Medicine

Sherry never liked me. Not until I got sick. Then she was always nice, at least when other people were around. I don't remember when I first got sick. One day I was fine, going to school and playing on my swing out back or with my dolls, and then my tummy was hurting. Whenever I would eat, my tummy would hurt me and I would get sick. Daddy was worried, but he had to work. So Sherry started helping take care of me. After a few days, I couldn't get out of bed. My legs were so heavy and my head made me feel like I had just gotten off of the merry-go-round. Everything was always spinning or tilting. I would get so dizzy I would just fall right down.

Daddy got scared and took me to the doctor. They made me pee in a cup and they took some of my blood. They told daddy they would have to put a camera in my belly. The doctor had me wear a mask that made me sleepy. When I woke up my throat was sore and the doctor said he couldn't find anything wrong. I started feeling a little better so they let me come home.

Then I got sick again. Daddy and Sherry took me to so many doctors, but no one could figure it out. Then one day the doctor looked sad and said he wanted to talk to daddy. Daddy was crying and Sherry looked sad. But I don't think she was really sad. I think she was just acting sad so daddy would feel better. Daddy said I was very, very sick and that they were going to take me home so I could be comfortable.

Two men brought in a new bed. It was just like the ones in the hospital, it had buttons to make it go up and down and to help me sit up. Sherry would try to give me soup without noodles in it. The clear tube coming out of my arm was always hooked up to bags of water.

AMANDA LEANNE

Sometimes a lady would come in and put something in the water and I would get sleepy, but my stomach would stop hurting.

Sherry told me I was dying and it was making daddy sad. She told me we could make daddy happy again if I took extra medicine, but we would have to keep it a secret. I asked her why, but she just shook her head and said it was better that way. Daddy would be even happier if it was a surprise. And when I was all better, we would tell him about the secret medicine.

I was so happy Sherry was nice now. She used to be so mean to me. She would throw my dolls in the trash and yell at me all the time. I would try to hide under my bed when I cried or she would get angry and spank me. She was always angry with me. I guess when I got sick; she must have thought that her being angry would make me sicker. Now she was so nice. And she was going to help me surprise daddy.

The secret medicine tasted bad though. I always throw up after she gives it to me. Sometimes it makes her angry face come back, but then she smiles and says the secret medicine is trying to get the bad sickness out of me.

Today my eyes won't open, my mouth won't work. I felt something being pushed in my mouth and tasted the nasty secret medicine. Daddy came home and has been sitting next to me crying. I want to tell him that it's okay, the secret medicine will make me all better. But I can't tell him anything. I don't know if I will be able to surprise him. I don't need the clear tubes anymore; I felt them take them out. I guess I don't need any medicine. Maybe I'm finally getting better.

I'm so tired though. All around is a heavy black blanket and it is keeping me warm. But it holds me down. I can't move. I think it's getting heavier. I can barely hear daddy anymore. I did hear Sherry.

"It'll be okay, there's nothing you could've done."

Something's Changed

The thud resonated through the house. Another slammed door following another quiet, tense evening. Lora nearly dropped her book but quickly regained her composure. She put the ragged end of an envelope in between the pages and put the book aside. Rubbing her palms along her cotton skirt did nothing for the sweaty, shaky feeling her hands seemed to keep recently. She moved quietly down the hall and toward the front door. As she eased her way outside, she spotted him on the porch smoking a cigarette. He did not even try to hide it from her. Stepping lightly she sat in the rocker near him and looked out over the wooded yard.

"You goin' to start bitchin' or bawlin'? Cuz really, I'm not in the mood for either one right now."

Lora straightened in the chair, blinking quickly to halt the tears.

"I really don't know what I am going to do. I think that's one of the problems."

He sighed, shaking his head and looking away. Another roundabout discussion, so it seemed.

"Why do we talk like this? Why don't you tell me what you feel the need to tell me, and then we leave it at that?"

Lora blinked harder and swallowed twice before she could find the words.

"Should we get a divorce?"

"Now why the hell we need to do that? You sleepin' around on me when I'm gone or somethin'?"

Now the hard blinks were more in surprise than to restrain the predictable onslaught of tears. Lora jumped up and began pacing the small porch.

"No, Jack. I would never do such a thing! I just don't understand why we should stay married if the day and a half that your home, every three weeks I might add, are going to be this tense and awkward. How is this even happening? We have almost twenty wonderful years together and now this? Was it the accident, Jack? Did something about that change your thinkin' about us?"

Lora spun and stared at her husband. Hurt, anger, confusion, fatigue. She really had no idea what was happening or why it was happening. Twenty wonderful years. Up until the accident, they even had a sex life that could put their high school years to shame. They had stayed up many nights talking about nothing and knew what each other was thinking half the time. Lora cooked meals they both loved and Jack always turned the tv to their favorite shows. They were happy, Lora thought, so happy. And then that damn accident.

Jack stared at the sun bleached wood beneath his boots. It was before the accident. That was when everything changed. Happiness and then the incident and now misery. Maybe he should have died.

"I don't know what happened. I guess something must have. Maybe I was supposed to die or something and now everything is off." He squinted in thought before shaking his head in frustration.

"You shouldn't say that. If you were supposed to die you would have." Lora tried to catch his gaze and he finally returned the pained look. "So what do we do, Jack? I love you, more than my life I love you. I just don't know if my nerves can keep this up."

"I know, and I don't blame you for feeling that way. Maybe you should find someone who will take care of you and show you more emotion than I can. I don't know if I can try to be better or not."

Jack fell silent, his gaze wandering back out to the trees casting their elongated shadows on a rock strewn yard. Lora swallowed back the lump that threatened to pour out, the gasping she felt her breast heave for. She turned and went back into the house. In the kitchen, she leaned against the sink, looking out the window, but not her eyes not really seeing anything. The sobs choked up, she felt the tears running down her cheeks like the warm trail of a finger. Her heart felt cold and her mind fuzzy and confused. She would never leave Jack. Jack would probably never leave her either.

Jack felt the weight of guilt on his shoulders. He was surprised he even still had a job. He was even more surprised he still had a wife, but that was a different kind of surprise. But he felt so numb. He remembered the accident, the yelling and screaming of the men in the work yard. He remembered the barely discernible bump of the truck as the tires crushed the dumb kid beneath their massive weight. They told him it wasn't his fault. Everyone there saw the stupid boy run from behind the dumpster and directly in front of his truck. Just as he was getting back up to speed, never reaching the black glossy numbers posted on the sign. The kid was barely out of high school, drunk on the job, supposed to be cleaning up garbage, and he ran in front of a damn semi. His life was over and Jack felt as if he was heading that same route. He never saw the boy and only knew what he looked like from the picture in the news. No one blamed Jack, which was rare. Usually they always said it was the trucker's fault. Too tired on the job, driving too fast, not looking around, or some other shit was always thrown up in the air. Apparently the kid had made enough dumb decisions in his life that no one pointed at Jack.

But no one asked Jack either. No one asked him if he was okay or if he felt different or if something had been wrong. Lora had tried, but he didn't want to tell Lora the truth. She didn't need to know how dead he felt. How dead he was. Lora didn't even realize how dead she was. He hadn't been paying attention that day. He hadn't even noticed the bump. The yells from the people who saw barely pulled him out of his stupor. Who let a man behind the wheel with so much on his head?

Yeah, he told them he was fine. He should have been dead then. He should have pulled the trigger the night before when he sat in his bunk with the revolver in his mouth. He didn't. Now a boy was dead, and he only wished he was.

Jack could hear Lora sobbing in the kitchen. He wanted to go to her, wanted to hold her and comfort her. He wanted to feel her in his arms again. He felt his own tears roll down his cheek in hot, fat drips. As the sobs built in his chest, he looked down at the photograph of him and his wife on their wedding day. His thumb moved lovingly over her face. He should have done it and saved the boy. Nothing says he wouldn't have gotten himself killed another way, though. He could have run out in front of one of the other dozen trucks coming out of there. He could have fallen off a damn tractor. But no, he had to run out in front of Jack. Jack, who should have pulled the damn trigger. Then he would be alive and Jack would be with Lora. Maybe he could touch her then. He thought about trying to tell her.

When he finally came home, after the accident and after the phone call, the lights were on. He thought some kids had broken into the cabin. Or maybe she had left them on and no one bothered to turn them off. He never told her there wasn't actually food on the table, there were no pots on the stove, she wasn't sweeping up any dust, and that she was never asleep in the bed with him. The bed was still cold, still empty. He should have pulled the trigger. Maybe he would know where she did sleep at night. If she slept at night at all.

Jack wiped his eyes with the back of his hand. It was the only way, the only way to be with her and to make her stop crying. No one should still be crying after they're gone. He loved her so much.

Lora wiped her face with the dish cloth when she heard the door open. She tried to breathe in and out slowly, calming herself, as she heard his boots move across the floor. Jack stopped at the entrance to the kitchen; he smiled at her under watery eyes. Her heart felt unbalanced, sad at his tears and joyful at that attempt to smile.

SHADOWS THROUGH THE FOG

"I think I'm going to run to the store and get some ice cream for after dinner. We can watch something on the tv and get brain freeze together."

"Alright. That sounds nice, Jack."

"I love you."

He smiled again and turned away, she listened as his footsteps faded out the door. A few hours later, Lora heard the door shut behind him as he came into the house. She finished fixing her hair in the mirror before heading downstairs to greet him. For the first time, since he came home after that accident, he pulled her to him and kissed her. She felt his mouth on hers and felt something inside of her sigh. Everything was going to be okay. They would get through this like they had gotten through so much more.

Jack was happy to be back home. He was happy to see his wife again. She seemed like a ray of sunshine. He couldn't remember what had happened earlier that day but he felt better about everything. He felt like they had moved into a better place and everything was going to be fine. He wasn't going to be leaving anymore, wouldn't need to be gone for weeks at a time. Jack and Lora could finally live their days in peace.

The house never sold, the stories alone scared most people. Anyone who tried to get close just felt overwhelming sadness. But the lights were always turning on and off and the doors opened whenever they wanted. Even water ran in the faucets, though everything had been disconnected. The landlord just let it be. It was a cabin in the mountains that was falling apart anyways. He had been sad when Lora had died from that aneurysm, all alone in there by herself. Then her poor husband, he was in that accident with that stupid kid. Poor guy must have gone over the edge mentally before he finally went over the edge for good. Drove his truck right off the side of the damn mountain. A part of him liked to think they were back together in that cabin, happy and living out their days as if nothing was amiss.

Dinner's at 7

The sun was already beginning to drop low in the sky, which was unfortunate when Danny was trying to drive west while occasionally glancing at the GPS on the dash. Mentally, he put another tick mark under the "cons" of agreeing to this dinner. The "pros" column was still winning, and the fact that he was over half-way to his boss' house was not wasted on him. There was no reason to chicken out now. Really, though, he knew it would be much more stupid to not go. The man had invited him personally. Seeing John Mavers walk into the kitchen of the bakery, his dark suit and slicked back hair quite the risk with the flour and sugar atomizing around him, had been a shock to Danny.

He had been busting his ass in the bakery for three years and knew that John Mavers owned several of the upscale patisseries. Slowly, Danny had been submitting ideas for adjusting recipes and creating his own delicate pieces in hopes of showing that he was more than just a dough-slinger. Danny wanted to show that he could make the business become something beautiful and unique with the artistically designed confections he had poured his heart into. In a last ditch effort to prove to the owner that Danny was truly onto something, he created a sample box of rich chocolate torts, delicate spun sugar flowers, beautifully molded truffles that exploded into exotic flavors when you bit into them, and several pastries bursting with fresh jams and topped with colored sugar crystals. He then personally took the box of his pride to the main office downtown and left it with Mavers secretary.

Danny hadn't honestly thought that Mavers would be impressed and was surprised the plump secretary with the perma-pissed expression didn't just eat it all herself. But John Mavers had been impressed. Apparently, unbeknownst to Danny, Mavers had been looking for someone with talent to turn the main bakery into a high class establishment with elegant and expensive desserts that would make every paper and social media market in, "or bigger!" as Mavers had expressed, arms thrown wide to match the grin on his face. Apparently his boss, who he hadn't met in person, was a pretty cheerful guy. His girth was a bit telling of his interest in the market of sweets, and his personality made him come off as cheerful and pleasant. So Mavers invited Danny to dinner at his residence to talk over a major promotion and the run of his own section in an upscale patisserie.

This was why Danny had to go. The reason Danny didn't want to go, other than the fact that he was nervous as hell about making a fool of himself in the home of a man that made more money than Danny could imagine, was the fact that he just didn't go to people's homes. Danny liked to go to his home, his quiet place that he kept immaculate and sparse. He had an OCD issue, and though baking and creating held it at bay, the moment Danny stepped out of the bakery, he would hurry to his car and head straight home. He hated the trash lying about, the people pushing and brushing their arms against him, the dirty shoe prints in the elevators, emptying takeout bags and coffee cups falling out of the open doors of cars, overflowing garbage, and really any mess left by another person. Going to someone's home where the possibility of filth, disorganization, being uncomfortable, or anything else was enough to throw Danny into a full blown anxiety attack. He had already had to do calming breathing exercises twice on his way to Mavers home. The problem embarrassed Danny and he usually kept it to himself. He wouldn't even visit his mother anymore, even though when she called she often pointed out the fact that he could be up to his elbows in powdered sugar and smeared melted chocolate all day but lose his mind if she had a few dirty dishes in her sink.

SHADOWS THROUGH THE FOG

One evening, though, that was it. A pleasant meal and some discussion and then Danny would be on his way to having freezers and fridges and pantries that he organized and controlled. The kitchen would be kept to his standards because he would be the mastermind bringing in the high paying customers. Danny hummed along to the radio, squinting against the sun, and listening intently for the GPS to tell him where his turn would be. His mouth slowly relaxed, the music soothing his frantic mind, until the automated voice announced that his next turn was on the right, where the large stone pillars on either side of the drive holding the massive black wrought iron gate as it sat open and awaiting his entry.

"In and out, chill, come one," Danny muttered, turning off the stereo with a flick of his hand, "one damn night, man, and my life is set."

He guided the car into the drive. The sun was no longer blasting his corneas, and as he blinked away the spots, the house came into view. He was actually expecting something bigger and a bit ridiculous. The house was large, bigger than the cookie cutter homes in the subdivisions, but not obnoxiously so. The drive made a loop in front of the house with a section off shooting to a two car garage on the side. The yard was well manicured, shrubs lining the front of the home and placed randomly amongst the well-tended oaks and maples. Splashes of bright color highlighted the property in subtle flower beds. Danny couldn't see much beyond the two story cream house, but he felt a little less stressed that he wasn't walking into a mansion. And if the yard was any indication, the family kept a clean and streamlined lifestyle.

Danny pulled around the drive and parked on the outer rim of the wide circle driveway. He made sure everything was off, gathered his cell phone and keys, and exited the car, making sure he locked it behind him. Walking up to the door, he felt his nerves begin to surface. This would be a wonderful night for him, as long as he could get through it without becoming a neurotic mess. The fact that he was thinking and worrying about thinking and worrying was an ironic issue to him. He felt a hysterical laughter trying to bubble up in his throat and did all he could to choke it down before reaching out to ring the doorbell.

He could hear the bell echo through the house, something thumped from deep within, but no other noises could be heard. Danny checked his cell phone to make sure he was on time. The boss had said dinner was at 7 and told Danny to arrive about a half hour early. His digital display told him it was 6:32PM. He wasn't early or late, so he didn't know what they hadn't answered. Hesitating a moment, considering the rudeness of him pushing the bell again so soon after the first attempt, Danny gave in and leaned his weight on the button, hearing the echo resonate back once more. He stood back and tried to keep from fidgeting, in case anyone checked through the peephole and saw a twitching nervous man on their porch. His mind began spinning with doubts. What if he was at the wrong house? What if the boss forgot and they were out to dinner or trying to figure out who the strange man on the porch was.

Danny sighed and felt a bit of relief, perhaps he wouldn't have to endure dinner tonight. Maybe they did forget or were gone or whatever. Being a regular baker at the patisserie wasn't all that bad; he didn't necessarily need the promotion. Plus, maybe the anxiety of the responsibility would take away from the enjoyment of the dream job. Danny nearly talked himself into leaving, having already backed up to the top of the steps when the door finally opened.

The woman was pretty; younger than Danny expected, but then again, when a man has money, his choice of women often had a wider range. She was pretty, dark brown hair pulled back into a ponytail, bright blue eyes, light make-up, and a warm smile. She was wearing a pair of jeans and a cream colored buttoned blouse with ruffled sleeves tucked in. Danny was a bit surprised, he expected a floral dress or slacks or something, something more adherent of a wealthy lifestyle.

"Hi, can I help you?" She looked Danny over, her smile slipping for a moment before locking it back in when she met his gaze.

"Uh, yes, sorry, I'm Danny Micheals. Mr. Mavers invited me to dinner this evening? At 7, is what he said?"

"Oh, yes, I'm sorry, it completely slipped my mind."

"Is Mr. Mavers not here?"

"No," she frowned and shook her head sympathetically, "he had some errands he needed to go do. He should be back by dinner. I would have thought he would tell me if we were having guests. I can have him reschedule with you."

"Oh, okay. I understand. I'm sorry if I bothered you. Just, please let him know I stopped by, I wouldn't want him to think I wasn't serious about the offer."

"The offer?" Her smile was slipping again.

"Yes, I, uh, well I don't know how much he told you," Danny could feel his palms getting sweaty, his nerves lighting up, "He really seemed to like my desserts and we had discussed me possibly having a position at the downtown patisserie."

"Oh, I see. Yes, I remember him mentioning that. He did talk about you quite a bit lately, in fact."

The woman, Mrs. Mavers presumably, glanced behind her at some unknown distraction before turning back to Danny.

"You know, why don't you come in and I can get you something to drink in the parlor while you want for John?"

"I don't want to intrude, if he forgot, I would rather not bother him."

"Oh nonsense. Come on in."

She stood to the side and waved Danny in. He wiped his palms on his pants, taking a deep breath before nodding, giving her a tight smile, and entering the home. The entryway opened up with a staircase to the right, an archway into the living room, or parlor, on the left, and the kitchen ahead. There were several shut doors through the hall, possible restrooms or closets, maybe even a study. Danny found himself speculating more about what he couldn't see than focusing on what he could. He nearly jumped when Mrs. Mavers lightly touched his elbow and led him into the living room.

"Just in here. Can I get you anything to drink? I have water, white wine and red wine, orange juice..."

"Water is fine, thank you."

Her smile seemed to be made of wax, melting randomly before sliding back into pace. Though the house was immaculate and tastefully decorated, Danny felt his anxiety building up. Something unnerved him about the odd woman, though pleasant she seemed, and he couldn't figure out what it was.

"Do you need any help or anything?" He wanted to seem polite and generous, in case Mrs. Mavers was just as uncertain and uncomfortable with him.

"No, no, just stay in here, I will bring you your water."

Danny nodded and tried to sit back on the chair, but immediately found himself sitting back on the edge and fidgeting. There was a nice fireplace in the living room, framed photos of an adorable blonde set of twins, one boy and one girl, through various frozen moments in their lives. Large potted trees sat in the corners of the room, a low table in the middle of the two chairs and couch with the entryway on one end and the fireplace on another. Danny supposed this would be the parlor, he didn't see any entertainment centers or televisions in the area that he would expect in a living room. He continued to fidget and was startled when the sound of a full glass clinked on the table. He had been looking at the photos when Mrs. Mavers sat down his glass of water.

"Darlings, aren't they?"

"Yes. I didn't know Mr. Mavers had twins."

"Yes, his two little angels."

"What are their names?"

"Uh, Jenny and Billy." She blinked hard at the photos, shook herself, and put her wax smile back on for Danny.

"Oh, those are nice names. Are they here?"

SHADOWS THROUGH THE FOG

"Yes, they're up in their rooms. You will probably meet them at dinner." Mrs. Mavers looked around, seemingly unsure of what to say or do.

"Are you sure Mr. Mavers won't mind me here, if he's forgotten the dinner and all?"

"Oh, I'm sure he would be much more embarrassed if he knew you had come and he had forgotten."

"Ah, I could understand that. Will he be much longer?"

"No, it should be soon."

She smiled and walked back out of the room. Danny wasn't sitting long before he began to fidget again. He picked up the glass of water and took a sip. There was a slight lemon flavor to the water, probably something to make it fresher, though the texture felt as if she used a powder that didn't dissolve quite enough. He appreciated the effort but didn't understand the point if you didn't use actual lemons. Though, what was he to say about how rich people hosted things. He didn't know what to expect, but he was a bit deflated to learn that Mr. Mavers hadn't told his wife about the dinner. Perhaps this wasn't going to go as well as he hoped. He continued to sip his lemon powdered water, inspecting every inch of the living room and trying not to feign too much boredom in case anyone walked back in without him noticing.

As his eyes scanned the photos on the mantle again, he felt himself sway a bit. He couldn't quite see the pictures as clearly. He tried to stand, suddenly his heart was racing and he felt unsure of what was happening. The living room tilted back and forth as if on a massive seesaw. He heard himself let out a groan, and suddenly Mrs. Mavers was at his side.

"Come on, Mr. Michaels, let's go sit in the dining room and wait for John."

Danny couldn't answer, his tongue felt heavy and swollen, the floor kept moving and walking did not seem like something he should be capable of. Could he walk? How do you walk? His mind began twisting and turning, getting cloudier and unsure. He was certain Mrs. Mavers would be able to tell something was wrong. She pulled one of his arms over her shoulders and guided him down the hall into the kitchen. The kitchen didn't seem right. This woman was not a clean cook. There were stainless steel dishes everywhere, and sauce and chunks of potatoes and meat were scattered on the counter top. Danny tried to focus on the mess, something wasn't making any sense. There was a pot of spaghetti sauce, thin angel hair noodles swirling on the top. Who made spaghetti and a meat and potatoes dish? Danny shook his head, trying to clear the murkiness. He wanted to examine the food, find out what she was making and how. The kitchen was his domain and this woman was butchering it.

She kept steering him on, pushing him forward until they entered the dining room. Mrs. Mavers pushed him down into a chair. He felt himself tilt, he knew he would not be able to sit upright, something was seriously wrong with him. He tried to get her attention, he kept staring at her, willing her to look at his face and know something was wrong. His confusion grew as he felt something tightening around his chest and arms. He had no strength, he couldn't lift up his arms to see what was on them and when he tried to look down he nearly spun his head like a head banger in slow motion.

"Now, now, sit still."

Mrs. Mavers was still hovering over him, doing something around him and behind him, the pressure became tighter. She was tying him up, helping him so he wouldn't fall over at the dinner table and embarrass himself. He wanted to thank her. She was very thoughtful and a very good hostess. He wanted to tell her these things but all he did was blow a raspberry, sputtering and spitting.

"Sh sh sh, dinner is almost done. John is here, see? The silly man was here the whole time."

Danny only then noticed that there were other people at the table. Mr. Mavers sat at the head of the table, his eyes half closed. He looked like he was asleep or at least falling asleep. But then his head bobbed as he began to try to lift it and look toward Danny. Something cold began running down Danny's spine, a feeling of ice setting into his veins. Something was definitely wrong with this. His vision was clearing a bit; whatever had been wrong seemed to be slowly going away. At least, it was going away in his head. His body felt even heavier, as if he was encased in cement. He took all his strength and lifted his head, quickly darting his eyes around to try to see everything he could at once.

He regretted the decision immediately. His gut spun as his vision tilted even more, everything blurred, but he saw someone else was at the table, opposite of him, but one chair over, closer to Mr. Mavers. It was another woman; this one had blonde hair and was closer to Mr. Mavers age. She was in a floral top, perhaps a dress, and she was crying. Something stuck out of her mouth, a rag or some other cloth. Danny's mind raced. As his vision settled from the motion of his head, Mr. Mavers and the other woman clarified. Both were sobbing, their faces red and wet. They had been at it for a bit. Mr. Mavers eyes met with Danny's, his brow furrowed and a new wave of sadness marred his face.

"Dinner's served!" the chipper voice of the woman that Danny was sure was NOT Mrs. Mavers, came carrying through the room.

She sat a large covered pot on the middle of the table between Danny, Mr. Mavers, and the woman that probably WAS Mrs. Mavers. Danny felt like he was going to vomit. He opened his mouth to try and speak but his words wouldn't come. His body was still immobile. Probably some paralyzing drug she put in the water. Mr. Mavers glared at the woman, a look of pure hatred on his face. Mrs. Mavers cried harder, trying to scream around the gag in her mouth, her glare darted between the woman and Mr. Mavers.

"I am so happy we could have a surprise guest. I was going to tell him to go, John, but it appears you have been making many promises to many people lately. I thought Danny should see how your promises affect people."

The woman's voice was still chipper, but hollowly so. As if she wasn't a person but something in the shell of a person. Danny didn't want her to take the lid off the pot. As his mind tried to go over the sights in the kitchen, a horrifying picture began to emerge.

"You see Danny, John made a promise to me as well. He promised me that he would make me his wife, that he would leave this ugly old hag and their little monsters and put me in a mansion. John promised he loved me. He promised to take care of me. And then do you know what he did, Danny? Do you?"

Danny tried to shake his head, he felt the water in his eyes begin to run over, the tears trialed down his face and he wanted to wipe them away, he wanted to run away.

"He lied. He broke his promises. This sorry sack of shit," Her voice began to get deeper, her face turning red as her mouth screwed in anger to spit every word out, her finger jabbing in Mr. Mavers direction, "He told the old hag about me, told her about his wandering dick problems, and they 'worked it out.' What the fuck? What about me?"

She crouched down, her face level with Mr. Mavers. Her nose wrinkled as she snarled at him.

"I didn't gag you old man. And that shit should be wearing off. You got anything to say yet? Huh? Did you tell the bitch about my baby? Did you tell her that her little angels weren't the only thing you sorry, saggy wrinkly pole shot out? Or were you afraid that she would want to know what happened?"

The woman glanced over at Mrs. Mavers, her face sliding back into the wax smile.

"I won't have pictures of my angel. Mine won't have golden curls or pretty smiles. My child is dead! He paid me to kill my child!"

"Ab....aborsh...aborsh.."

"Yes, an abortion. He paid for me to have an abortion. Murder. That money was blood money. He gave me that money to pay for broken promises and the murder of my child."

SHADOWS THROUGH THE FOG

She stood up and walked around to Mrs. Mavers' other side.

"But now my baby won't be alone. My little boy can play with his half-siblings. Won't that be nice, Mary? Our children, playing together?"

Mrs. Mavers choked around the gag, muffled screams from her red, tear stained face. Mr. Mavers eyes widened, his face shaking, the red of anger sliding into the white green of illness. The girl grabbed the handle of the pot and whipped the lid back, throwing her other hand up into the air.

"Ta-da! See, I'm a great cook too! I could work in your fancy bakery! I can be useful!" She looked at the pot, the two rounded shapes peeking out of the red liquid, the bloodied hair mostly matted down. Hair, not spaghetti. Angel hair, but not pasta. "Look at that! Now, I was only expecting two for dinner, so one of you will have to share."

Danny felt the world shift. A gray shade was pulled over his eyes, his stomach rolled, and his chest buckled, he felt the vomit rolling out of his mouth and pouring down his chest. He tried to move his body but everything still felt so heavy. John Mavers bucked; a sound like the shrieking of a bobcat began bubbling from deep in his throat, his face red and bloated with eyes bulging. Mrs. Mavers sobs shook her whole body, she was convulsing, the gag falling out of her mouth and her screams getting louder and louder as the cloth fell away. The smell now overwhelmed Danny. The coppery sweet odor of blood and raw meat, the tangy smell of sweat and piss, and the acrid scent of vomit. He tried to breathe in through his mouth and began choking on his own vomit.

The woman sat in the seat next to Mrs. Mavers, across from Danny. She frowned, looking at the three of them. She sighed heavily and then picked up a large ladle. She dipped it into the pot, under one of the heads, and used her hand to balance it on the utensil as she pulled it up and sat it in the large salad plate in front of Mr. Mavers before repeating the procedure with the other head. She scooped the bloody mess, bits of unknown matter, probably bone pieces, not potatoes, and ladled it on top of each head. She looked at Danny and shrugged.

"Neither one of them likes to share much, so you're out of luck."

Danny felt more vomit coming up as he tried to suck in air and catch his breath from the burn of choking. Immediately he inhaled as his body regurgitated, filling his lungs. He sucked in air to no avail, unable to breathe out enough to get the mess out of his chest. He heaved and tried to breathe, tried to pull in something or cough out something else. No matter how hard he tried, the breaths pulled smaller and smaller and the gray began to get darker. As a black curtain descended over his vision he heard the woman telling the Mavers that she had made a wonderful dessert for them as well, as long as they ate all their dinner.

Death'll Do You Part

Kevin slumped down at his desk, the computer screen was starting to look like one of those old pictures you had to cross your eyes or go out of focus to make out. He tried that, it made it worse. His head was pounding, his back hurt, and he really could have been anywhere but here. And home, probably not home either. Kevin sighed, rubbing his head in frustration, and sat up to try to make sense of the words on the screen. As he forced himself to focus, he slid back into the monotony of another day on the grind.

At 7 he figured he had stretched the day as long as he could, and grabbed his satchel. He didn't know why he carried it. It was black leather, it looked professional, but other than containing bottles of warm water, crushed granola bars, a novel he would probably never finish, and a few pens, there wasn't really much use for it. But Jen had gotten it for him on their seventh or eighth anniversary. Back when the marriage was cooling down, but still felt like something, still had life. Kevin shook his head and walked out to the car. Tossing the bag in, he slid in and cranked the ignition.

...hundred divorces. I mean, you have to see the boom in donated organs and the Cinder Corporation.

I agree with that, Dave, I just don't understand how love leading to murder is commonplace. Years ago people signed papers, split their things, and went their own ways.

Kevin shook his head in disgust as he turned off the radio. He eased his car into the turn off lane, his mind elsewhere. He could see the dark clouds over the local Cinder Corporation facility. He wondered how many bodies went through there every day. He knew some areas were still trying to burn all of the people that had been dug up and the families were willing to pay for their ashes and remains. Imagine that stick in your craw. You paid thousands of dollars to put grandma in a pretty box inside a cement box in the ground with a slab of marble on top and the government decides no more cemeteries, digs her up and burns her and charges you for her ashes. It was fucked up.

The whole world was fucked up. Overpopulation was a serious issue. If you were diagnosed terminal, you had a week to say your goodbyes and get your shit together before the government came and euthanized you before crisping you up with the leading private company of death, Cinder. There were food shortages, child limits on households, and no more adoptions and orphans, not that the government would admit where those kids were. I'm sure Cinder gave the government discounts on smaller bodies.

His stomach rolled, as he turned onto his street. The houses were small, compact, simple designs for simple families. Since he and Jen never had kids, they got a one bedroom home. It had a kitchen, bathroom with a standing shower, and a small living area. If they had kids, they would have lived two roads down or further, where the two bedroom homes were. He wasn't sure if it was a good or bad thing that they didn't have any.

At first, it wasn't for a lack of trying. Then he realized he was going nowhere with his company, no higher pay meant it would be much harder to afford the increase in house payments for the bigger home and the monthly fee for having a child, not to mention the cost of more clothing, food, and everything else. Jen loved her art. She painted daily. Sometimes they had really good months where she would sell a big piece and they would have twice the income, then they could go almost a year or more with her not making anything. Then they would live paycheck to paycheck on Kevin's shit pay.

Shoving the car into park, he yanked out the keys and glared at the green front door. Now he was thinking a kid would have been worth the money, the investment. He thought he still loved her and that she loved him, but they never talked. He couldn't remember the last time he had kissed her. Sex, sex was a faint memory. They smiled at each other, they didn't fight, but after fifteen years, something had dulled. At least they made their promises long ago. They wouldn't divorce. Their agreement was unless one of them was guilty of abuse or adultery, they would not divorce.

He couldn't imagine divorcing her, displaying their failure in front of the world while one of them paid with their life. Maybe it was his fault, maybe he just wasn't trying hard enough. But when you're with someone so long, you know when they want you to kiss them, hug them, and make them feel good, and you know when they want you to just leave them alone. He couldn't remember how long it had been since Jen wanted anything but to be left alone.

Kevin pushed the door open and grabbed his satchel. He let out a deep sigh as he walked up to the front door. Shoes and bag both were tossed to the side of the entryway as he headed to the kitchen. Checking the microwave, he grabbed the plate and sat at the table in the dark. Ten minutes of picking at his food and he knew he was eating tonight either. As he dumped the contents of the plate into the trash, he noticed several cans of some kind of protein shake.

"I didn't hear you come in." Jen was standing in the doorway in a tank top and some kind of sporty looking shorts. Far from her normal attire of flowy skirts and dresses.

"I didn't know if you were working or not so I didn't want to bother you."

"Dinner taste bad?"

"Uh, no, no, it was okay, I just, feeling a little under the weather is all."

She nodded, her facial expression never changing. Without another word she turned and walked away, her long blond hair was in a ponytail, but it wasn't as long anymore. He noticed she had cut it up close to her shoulders. Different hair, clothes, and protein shakes, he had no clue who she was anymore. Shit, he didn't know who he was anymore.

For the first time in his life, Kevin felt nervous about his marriage. Everything was okay, as long as they could keep pushing through together, but maybe at 32 Jen wanted to try to move on. It would make sense. Before one of the guys at work was served his divorce, his wife started working out, trimmed her hair and nails, and completely changed. He had no clue until they came to get him. He wasn't prepared. But Kevin couldn't just ask her, he would have to wait and watch. If she kept working out, kept getting more distant, then he would have to do the same. He would need to prepare.

Before heading to bed, he spent thirty minutes in the bathroom vomiting up mostly froth before cleaning his face and staring in the mirror, the horror of what was happening finally setting in.

KEVIN'S STATE OF MIND went through a drastic change as he noticed the changes in Jen. He began to leave work at four instead of staying late and hit the local gym. If she was going to serve him, he would be prepared. She never showed any emotions anymore, her face always expressionless and voice flat. The pain and betrayal began to evolve within Kevin as he focused on himself for the first time in years. As the weeks went by, he felt better about himself, stronger and more in control of his life, than ever before. He would win the divorce and he would find a better way to live. He would live for him and no one else. Never again would he trust another person or give them the he had given Jen. The power she thought she could use to destroy him.

He hid his slimming waistline and flatter stomach, keeping his clothing loosely tucked in. He paid for the gym with cash instead of the card. He ate healthy at work and didn't worry about Jen since she had stopped cooking for him after the night he noticed her shorter hair. As he grew stronger, his anger grew thicker. She promised him she wouldn't do it. They promised each other. But now he knew that promises were nothing, and so was their marriage.

AS THE DAYS AND THEN weeks passed, Kevin started to feel antsy. He was fit and ready to go, but Jen had not said anything, there had been no change for the better or worse and he felt like he was losing his mind. He had started gun training and taken up martial arts instead of going to the gym every day. His adrenaline was up, his blood boiling, and she was dragging it out. Maybe she was trying to do the same. Maybe she was trying to train in some crazy combat he hadn't thought about.

Then he came home and saw the envelope taped to the door. His name printed carefully on the front. He snatched the offending item from the door and shoved it in his satchel. As he opened the door, he released the envelope into the bag and felt around for the pistol. His hand closed around the cold metal grip. He looked at Jen, sitting on the couch as he brought out the gun. Her eyes widened in shock as he pointed it at her head and pulled the trigger twice. Her head jerked back, the wall spray painted in red behind her as she slumped to the side.

Kevin dropped the gun on the couch next to her and pulled out the envelope for the phone number to call when the divorce was served. There was one sheet of paper folded into thirds, and mechanically he flattened it and began to scan for a phone number when the realization of what it said finally hit him.

Jen typed it up on a computer, for some reason, and gave him that instead of talking to him. It was his fault, he had been just as distant if not more so.

AMANDA LEANNE

Kev,

Things have been so hard for us lately. We never talk, we never smile, and now I can't even cook something for you to eat. I know you work a lot to support us and it's wearing down on you. So I got a new job. I'm a yoga and meditation teacher at the spa downtown. I will be making twice what you are in half the time. So now you can cut back on your hours and have some relaxation time. I saved up my first few paychecks, and I was thinking we could go on a vacation. Maybe renew our vows and start over. A mid-life crisis, I suppose. I'm sorry it took this long for me to pull my weight. But I promise, things will be different now.

Love always and forever, til death do us part,

Your Jen

As the paper tumbled out of his hands, Kevin reached for the pistol. He only needed to pull the trigger once.

The Other Side of the Mirror

I'm worried. She wasn't there again this morning. Last time she wasn't there I had a mess to clean up in the basement. That wasn't the hardest clean up I had to do for her, but it was the closest I ever came to having the trouble come back on me. I can't tell them who she is and where she is, they wouldn't believe me.

I tried leaning up on my toes, smashing my face against the glass out of desperation. I angled myself every way I could think of, but I couldn't see her. So I got a screwdriver and tried to pry it off the wall. Maybe I could walk around backwards, staring into the mirror. Then I could find her. She has to be here. I don't think she can get too far, as long as I'm around.

Not that I know how it works.

All I know is sometimes when I look in the mirror, she isn't there. I just see whatever is behind me. I don't have a reflection. My reflection is someone else. It's her. And when she isn't there, somebody is dying.

But I'm not scared. I'm not angry. I'm not sad. I'm worried. If she is doing it again then I have to clean it up. She always leaves a mess on my side. At least she keeps them, whoever they are, on her side. I never see them, but I never find a body either.

So where is she today? What is she doing? Who is she hurting? Why?

I try not to think about it. I go about my day and do what I do.

That night she's back. I see her, the faint smile on her lips, the tiny almost imperceptible dark red dots near her hair line and one on her cheek bone. She winks. I smile weakly. I still haven't found the mess. I know it's here.

I sigh, shaking my head at her. She mocks me, shaking her head too. Exaggerating the sigh.

The mess is in my bed. There is blood everywhere. I groan in frustration as I start pulling up the corner sheets, wrapping everything together and bundling it tightly. I don't know how I will get rid of it this time.

SHE'S NOT IN THE MIRROR again. Second day in a row. Highly unusual.

I start trying to pry the mirror off of the wall again. I can't get it to pull away. I chip at the paint, at the drywall, but the mirror won't come off. I don't see her.

I stare at the mirror, where she should be, where she pretends to be my reflection.

My chest hurts, it burns. I look down, there is blood on me. A red, wet bloom explodes from my chest in one spot, and then three, then so many I can't count. Each new stain brings with it a wave of pain. I try to breathe. I can't. It hurts so much. I look up to see if she is watching, to see if she is here.

She is standing there, pretending to be me, except she has a knife. She smiles as she pushes into my stomach again and again. I want to ask her why. I want to know what I did. All I did was clean up after her.

The world gets fuzzy, the black is slowly filling up everything. The last thing I see is her watching me, her own shirt bloodied, the knife in her hand, and tears pouring down her cheeks.

I feel the cold floor slam into me and hear the knife clatter on the tiles next to me as the world ends.

Daryl Had an Idea

Daryl had an idea. As with many of his ideas, there was a maniacal brilliance in which it was based upon, but it had several obvious flaws.

"You realize the likelihood of these things blowing up is really high? I mean, like, probably going to happen?"

"That's a risk, sure. But so is people walking around glued to the damn things. When's the last time you shut yours off?"

"I dunno," I couldn't help that my hands rubbed the shiny protected screen, watching the swirl of colors as I swiped and my home background lit up with greens and blues of a crazy fluorescent 3-D shroomland. "I mean, man, I get it. I get annoyed at myself. I go to lie down in bed and I check my phone. If it blinks, I grab it. If it vibrates, I grab it. I check it before I sit up in the mornings. I take it to the shitter. I mean, yeah, I'm a bit attached. Is it a bad thing? I don't know."

"How are you even asking that? Check the weather; check your email once or twice a day. Look up an address or phone number. Those are great, fantastic!" Daryl threw his hands up, pacing back and forth in my shitty little living room, "But staring at it seventy percent of the time your eyes are even open"

"It's not that much. You're exaggerating."

"It's enough that people are ramming their cars into each other, children are drowning and walking into traffic right in front of their mothers, kids don't know how NOT to cheat in school anymore, and it's even starting to get a wave by when you rudely do it when people are fucking talking to you!" I barely heard the words as my phone was slapped out of my hand.

"Dude, you need to seriously chill. And as much as you hate it, I paid a lot for it. I also need it to call people, get texts, check in with work, and do a shit ton of other stuff. So fuck off, man." I couldn't help but shake my head, brows raised at his crazy land.

"I'm just saying, people need a reason to not touch them for a bit. You been surfing the web for thirty minutes? Cool, you're done. The phone heats up and isn't tolerable to hold in your sweaty little hand or against your damn head. After an hour or so, it cools down slowly and then you can use it for another thirty minutes."

"And what if someone gets an emergency call or text or something?"

"They can still touch it, it just won't be pleasant."

"So they stick it in their pocket or purse and either get the shit burned out of them or they end up blowing something up. Or the battery overheats and the phone BLOWS UP!"

I don't know why I tried arguing with him. It's always something. The dude gets on a bender about something he hates or can't state or some new "low aspect of human society" and loses his shit, for real. I mean, he's mad smart, crazy smart, but crazy is the key word here.

"You aren't listening."

"No, I am, and I have a phone in my hand while I'm doing it. This will cause damage and death and bad things and just no."

"The government can already do it, you know? Built in people-problem-solver. Country goes nut up and they push a button and the phones go kapewy and that is it. All I'm saying is use the physical detriment to make people wake the fuck up and explore the world around them a bit. Check and see what the color of the sky is before seeing what everyone thinks the newest color the sky should be if it had rights to be whatever color it wanted."

I couldn't help but laugh. Daryl glared at me, his face sweaty and eyes wide. It truly amazed me how someone so intelligent could allow passion to color the world around them. He was so easily blinded by aggression and hate, frustration and inability to understand people. He was a sociopath, that I was sure of. Possibly narcissistic and a tad psychopathic. His ideas would make a great movie, but if the dude ever got further than our bodunk town, I kind of feared what he would get into. That fear saved my life. But as crazy as he is, I think I'm just a coward.

"I'm on to something, man. You know it, you just don't want to agree. You know that people need to wake up. If everyone was limited, if everyone was forced to set down their phone or tablet or whatever, the online noise and traffic would die out and people would pay attention to each other and the world around them."

"At the risk of exploding."

"Dude, fuck off."

Daryl stomped out the door, slamming it behind him. At least he shut it this time. I shook my head, picked up my fiendish device and checked my notifications. Dude has a point, though.

I DON'T KNOW WHAT'S scarier; knowing your friend comes up with these ideas, knowing he is capable of carrying out these ideas, or knowing he makes up so many of them you forget about them. Until one day, when I'm checking my messages from this chic on some app, staring at her photo shopped and filtered tits taken at some obscure angle, my phone started feeling a bit warm. I closed the apps and programs to the home page, checked the stats, like that would tell me anything, and took the case off. Just as my finger went to touch one of the vibrant blue little icons, I realized it was getting hotter.

"What the fuck?" I dropped it on the couch, flipped it over, popped off the back cover and used my finger to flick the battery out of position.

AMANDA LEANNE

I knew some of the games would cause the little bastard to get hot, especially if it was plugged in, but it damn near hurt to even touch it. I reached down and poked the phone, it was still pretty hot, but I figured without the battery, cool was the only direction it could go. I shrugged, shaking my head in frustration, and headed to the kitchen to grab a beer.

As I walked back to the living room, I could see the tiny tendrils of smoke and then heard a loud bang, an explosion. I found myself falling to the floor, hands jerking above my head soaking me in ice cold beer.

"Mother fucker!" Scrambling out of the wet floor, I half-crawled half-lunged into the living room.

My couch was on fire.

Where the phone had been was now a black hole, right through the piss yellow foam. The blue fabric fading to black as it encircled the gaping maw remaining. My mouth dropped open, I was in shock. It was only then I thought of Daryl. The last time I had seen him, five years before, and the last insane rant he was going on about. Cussing more than was really necessary, I raced outside. There was no other car than my little white sedan, no vehicles other than mine, no one on the road. I ran around the house, ducking to look under bushes and trees. There was no one anywhere around my house.

Scratching my head, I felt an ache building. I needed to go straight to the cell phone store and hand them the burnt remains of my couch cushions and ask for my $600 back for the phone, a new couch, and, well, another new phone.

As I walked back in, the cushions were starting to really ignite. The chemicals and plastics burst with the heat. I grabbed the edge of the one closest to me and chunked it out the door. Burning the shit out of myself, I threw the other two out, nearly catching myself and the carpet on fire. I grabbed some ratty towel off the floor to smother the back of the couch. Black soot streamed up my wall, a star pattern on the ceiling above where my phone had been. One cushion was really just the outer edges. If that thing had been in my hand or pocket, I would either be wishing I was dead or granted the wish.

I grabbed my keys and looked around for my cell phone when I glanced back at the couch. Never fucking mind.

Rage filled me as I stepped over the smoldering remains of the cushions and got to my car. As I opened the door, I heard two loud bangs from the house across the street. I heard Mrs. Lorence screaming and Mr. Lorence yelling something. I ran toward the house, didn't even look as I shot across the street. I could see smoke through the screened door.

"Mr. and Mrs. Lorence?"

I could barely hear me over them. Mr. Lorence was yelling a mixture of cuss words and screams for help. Mrs. Lorence had died to a whimper and then just a moan. As I yanked the door open, I saw Mrs. Lorence in her pink recliner. Her chest, face, and half way up her forearms were a mass of blood and black, smoking fragments of her gown sticking to the edges. Mr. Lorence came stumbling around the corner, tripping over his pants. One ankle was still in one leg of them, the rest of the pants trailed behind. His hands were bloody nubs and from his face down to his knees was a bloody black mess. He had been on the toilet.

I stood frozen, unsure what to do. Mrs. Lorence wasn't making a noise or moving, didn't even look like she was breathing. Mr. Lorence waivered before falling on the ground face first and convulsing, moans and groans of agony reverberating around me. Trying to pay attention to where I was going and not squeezing my eyes shut, I jumped over him to the kitchen and grabbed the yellow corded phone. Mrs. Lorence insisted they had one. I helped them install it.

The dial tone was a foreign and yet welcomed sound in my ear. I dialed 911 and waited as the line trilled and the clicks of an answer came through.

AMANDA LEANNE

"We are experiencing an abnormal amount of phone traffic. Please hang up and try again."

I did. Twice. Even a third time as I looked around the edge of the kitchen wall and glanced at the two bodies. Mr. Lorence could still be alive, but I didn't know. I didn't want to know. Dropping the phone, I jumped over his motionless body and ran out the door. As soon as I was sitting in my car, my brain froze. Where should I go? What should I do? Did Daryl do this? Did he kill people? Or what if, by some crazy coincidence, Daryl's government conspiracies were on point?

I turned the key, and slowly eased out of the driveway. I wanted to find help, but what if the help wouldn't be pleased to see I had survived? Not that everyone's phones would kill them. Not everyone could possibly be holding their phone at the exact moment that they blew up. So what was the point? And my phone was a different type than the Lorence's. Not the same phone or company.

My frustration was just growing. Lost at what to do, I decided to head to Daryl's mom's house. I had no clue where Daryl had been or where he was, but maybe she could tell me, and then he could tell me what the fuck was happening.

Immediately I realized that I had not thought the whole traveling aspect through. Good thing Ms. Thomas lived on a backroad. I still had to cross the hard road to get to her street, and the devastation was immediate. Cars sitting still, smoking, red and black splashes on the windows. Two cars intertwined down the street, a few random ones in the ditches, the trees on the side, facing the wrong way on the street. Smoke and the smell of burning filled the air. Screams faintly rang out from some of the vehicles. One girl was stumbling around, holding her right elbow, nothing left beneath but a drizzle of blood and pieces of flesh.

Hitting the accelerator, I darted across and eased my way around the winding roads, dodging stopped cars and bloodied people. Some walking, some lying in the road. My mind was starting to shut it out.

SHADOWS THROUGH THE FOG

My focus was finding Daryl. If he had done this, I didn't know what I would do, honestly. I was in a gray zone. The world was static around me. My goal was the little white and blue house, the woman inside, her son, and maybe some answers.

I pulled down the long drive, moss hung from the oaks on either side, obscuring the view. I wasn't even sure it was the right house, I wouldn't know until I had seen it, and I didn't remember the trees being this overgrown.

As I began to second-guess myself, the house came into view. The algae had been a small issue years ago, but now the house was more green than white. The blue was sun bleached to a gray tone, marred by more algae growing in the cracks and edges of the rectangles on either side of the smudged windows. What I definitely did not recognize was the shiny metal camper to the side. Its exterior littered with antennas. Daryl's old black car that sat crouched near the back end of the building.

I pulled up next to the building, my stomach churning. Would I find him maimed, dead, or smiling in evil glee? My hands shook as I reached for the round metal knob. I thought about knocking but figured now was as good a time as any to dismiss formalities. The door opened, unlocked, and I stepped inside. Daryl, I presumed, sat at a computer chair in front of five different types of monitors, stacked and zip-tied to a rig on one wall of the camper. A small pile of dirty laundry, from the smell, and blankets sat at the far end. Cans, plastic wrappers, and paper take out bags littered every available surface.

Sitting in front of the glowing screens, his head in his hands, a mass of wildly tangled hair obscuring his face, was Daryl.

"Hey? Daryl?"

The man jumped, his head snapping in my direction. Blood and tears poured down his face. I didn't see any wounds or blackened flesh, no burning plastic.

"What the fuck..."

"You were right. I'm so sorry. You were right. And momma never listened, never! Why wouldn't she listen?"

I shook my head, slowly putting it together. She had a phone. He probably told her all his whack job theories, but nowadays, you needed a phone. She had one, and it exploded. It was her blood.

"Did you do this?"

His face dropped, he stared at the screens. Lines of data, maps with colored circles. He began shaking his head, slowly at first, and then faster.

"They should have put them down when they got warm. Who doesn't put them down?"

He glanced at me, my hands, my chest.

"You put it down?"

"Of course I put it down. It got hot as fuck instantly. You blew up my phone? Your mom's phone? The Lorences are dead, by the way, you fucking psycho piece of shit!"

"I found the government program. It existed! It did! I didn't have to do anything but flip a switch, a line of code, set it off and now..."

My mind whirled, my world spun. The psycho little fucker had attacked the country. Killed so very many. Kids playing on phones, old people, stupid people, businesses, everything, how far did it go?

I thought about the fact that he almost killed me. That I should have died too.

I walked up to him, staring at his stupid fucking face. I grabbed his hair in a tight handful and slammed his face into the keyboards in front of him. And again, and again. One of the monitors fell, gaining a blow to the back from his face. He didn't even fight. I kept slamming his head until my hand yanked away, hair still twined around my fingers, blood sprayed on the monitors still standing, the table, the garbage, my clothes. I screamed at his gurgling limp body. Kicked his chair and ran out the door.

SHADOWS THROUGH THE FOG

The world was going to be a mess. And my stupid best friend was the one that did it. I shook my head, walked to my car and went home.

When the Chains Snap

The porcelain tile was ice under her feet. The plastic toilet seat was almost as cold as she felt it through the thin fabric of the threadbare nightgown. Fake silk, itchy lace, and straps a light yank away from completely ripping. She should have left the light off, but then he would have come to see what she was doing. With it on, he could assume she was using the bathroom. If it took a bit, maybe he would think she was going number two and he would be even more reluctant to walk in. She hoped. She wished. If she was religious, she would have prayed.

Her elbows rested in her palms, arms crossed over her chest. Goosebumps had broken out across her skin, giving it a grainy feel. Her hair hung in front of her face, blurry clumps of brown beyond her tear filled eyes. Her teeth bit into her lip, as she choked back the sobs. Another wave of shivers raced down her neck and the length of her spine. Her eyes would be red, puffy, bloodshot. He would know she had been crying. If he didn't walk in and witness it himself, that is.

In the distance, beyond the closed door and down the hall, the muffled giggles of the toddler. The deep baritone of her husband's voice seemed to vibrate through the walls. The giggles increased, changed and morphed into squeals of laughter. As comforting as the sound should have been, a new wave of despair crashed over her. She shoved her fist into her mouth, biting down on her knuckles as her body jerked with the near soundless sobs. The ground rumbled as her husband roared in laughter. A growl bubbled in her throat, thick and viscous as it maneuvered through the sobs and into her throat.

AMANDA LEANNE

    She began rocking, back and forth, the pain in her bones and muscles and blood sizzled through her body. The tiles melted under her feet, the walls began to crumble. Her eyes focused on the mirror, the reflection of the framed cheap flower painting taking center stage. The gaudy gold trim and contrasting jewel and pastel tones swirled into themselves, spinning into a puddle reminiscent of vomit. The puddle didn't drip, it clung to the ugly peach paint. The mirror began to warp and buckle, distorting the image further. The sharp corners, dull and spotted from age, began to curl in under the invisible flames of the room. The paint on the walls began to bubble, darkness creeping in as the heat burned through.

    Darkness. She squeezed her eyes shut, embracing the black behind her lids. The static roar of the fire died down, faded. Sucking in her breath, she slowly opened one eye, and saw the hideous painting was whole and still hanging above the toilet, behind her on the wall. The mirror was flat and still, and the walls were not burning. The tiles were no longer cold, but not hot either. Her body heat had warmed them under her unmoving feet.

    As she pulled her fist away from her mouth, she saw trails of red where her teeth had broken the skin. Her body shook as she pulled in one ragged breath after another. The room felt small, the walls were too close. She barely had time to stand, spin around and open the lid of the toilet as she fell to her knees, heaving what little she had eaten into the clean, white bowl. Her chest ached and her stomach cramped as her body convulsed, emptying her stomach completely. She almost feared feeling her insides being shoved up and out as the dry heaves finally began to taper off.

    Her sweaty head dropped onto the cool plastic of the seat. She took some comfort in knowing she had cleaned the toilet only a few hours earlier. The world faded into grays and back to jarring color as a sharp pain started behind her eyes. Her ears rang and buzzed. She braced herself on the flimsy seat, trying to keep from falling over onto the floor, although that had been cleaned as well. Cleanliness didn't make the tile much softer for her head if she did fall, though.

Exhaustion poured through her. She wondered if she would be able to stand. Her legs felt like warm jelly. Muffled footsteps came from the distance, getting louder as they approached the bathroom. Her eyes darted to the crack under the door. The bedroom was dark, so she couldn't see his shadow. He was standing there, she knew he was. He was listening, waiting to hear the sounds of splashes from the toilet or the spray of a shower head.

"Jennifer?" The knob wiggled as he attempted to open the door. "Jennifer, are you okay?"

Her throat was sore, dry and burning. She tried swallowing the acrid taste that enveloped her tongue.

"Jennifer!" The knob jiggled ferociously, the door vibrated as his fist banged into the hollow wood.

"I..." she coughed, wincing in pain, "I'll be out in a minute."

"Are you okay?" He was trying to sound concerned. He wanted her to open the door.

"Yeah, um," coughing, she tried to clear the hoarseness from her voice, "I must have eaten something that didn't sit well."

"At dinner? Jack and I had the same thing you did. Are you sure?"

"I don't know. Maybe it's a bug or something. I'm fine, I'll be out in a minute." Her words were rushed, almost frantic.

"Okay. I'm gonna lay Jack down for the night. I'll come check on you when I'm done. You want some water or something?" He was convinced. He was suspicious.

"No." Her voice broke slightly. He was still standing there, waiting.

After a moment, the thumps of him heading away from the bathroom gave her a sigh of relief. Reaching up with her leaden arm, she pushed down on the chrome handle, ignoring the tiny flecks of icy water and vomit that misted from below her. She turned over, on her hands and knees, and crawled the short distance to the sink, grabbing the edge of the Formica counter to pull herself up. She stared at her reflection. Her eyes were wild, red rimmed and glassy. Turning on the faucet, she scooped cold water into her hand and splashed it into her mouth. Swishing and spitting she repeated a few times before leaning over, bending at a painful angle, and gulped the cool liquid down her burning throat.

The freshly laundered blue rag was soaked through and then rubbed vigorously on her face. Strength was easing back into her muscles, her legs still weak but no longer rubbery. She ringed out the rag and draped it over the front of the sink. Looking into her own eyes, she took deep breaths in, slowly releasing and then back in again. Pulling in the calm, is how she pictured it. She ignored the flames flickering at the bottom of the mirror. She refused to look at the painting as it began to blur. Deep breaths.

"Jennifer?"

She jumped. She hadn't heard him coming back. He could be like that, when he wanted to. Stealthy and sneaky. Her eyes darted to the dark green shower curtain. Something moved behind it. Her mouth tightened as she frowned, watching carefully for the next flicker. There it was, a ripple from the back. It wasn't enough to rattle the hooks hanging on the rod above, subtle but she saw it.

"Jennifer? You're kinda of worrying me. Unlock the door."

Her eyes narrowed as she stared at the sheet of plastic, the shadowy dips between the waves as it fluttered again.

"Goddamnit Jennifer!" He wasn't yelling, but he was angry. His voice low and deep, growling at her. "I will break the damn door down."

"I'm fine. I'll be out shortly."

"What the hell?" The knob jerked and jiggled, the door vibrating as he banged against it.

"Please, please just go away. I'm a mess. I'll be out in a minute."

"Jennifer, what is going on?" The sound of his fist hitting the door caused her to jump back.

SHADOWS THROUGH THE FOG

"Please!" Her voice came out a hoarse yell, not quite a scream. "Go away!"

The walls bubbled as if they had liquefied. The mirror softly creaked as hairline cracks began racing across its surface. The tiles wobbled in loose grout.

Her sobs came out loud and thick as she hugged herself, sinking down to the floor. The ceiling bowed above her as if she was the source of gravity. The shower curtain shook and jerked on the plastic rings. Once again she shoved a raw fist into her mouth, biting down on the knuckles and sending a trickle of coppery flavor into her gasping mouth.

The door exploded inwards, the toddler cried from his room, and her husband stood above her, his breath heaving in and out as he stared at her. His eyes were unnaturally wide, seeming to get bigger the longer she watched. His teeth elongated, poking out of his parted lips as yellow stained spears. The hair on his body was thick, disgustingly so. His hands gnarled claws.

"Jeeennnnifeerrr!" His mouth opened to reveal the full rows of shark-like teeth as he roared her name.

She screamed into her fist, her body shaking uncontrollably, tears streamed down her face in torrents blurring the room around her as it continued to deteriorate. They would both die if it kept going.

His words garbled into unintelligible growls and snarls. She pulled herself backward, the knobs of the cabinet poking painfully into her spine. She dropped her hands to her side to push against the floor, wanting to push straight through the thin wooden doors, into the cabinet, through the wall, out into the world and away from the hell that was encapsulating her.

His hands came up, reaching for her as he came closer. The bloody cloven hooves cracking the tiles with each step. Jennifer continued to scream as the world pulsed in and out, the colors getting brighter and dimmer as it all swam together. And then finally, the black rolled in and coated her vision, muffled her ears, and pulled her away from the demon.

BEFORE HIS HANDS COULD grab her shoulders, she seized up, her body jerking hard twice, and then collapsed onto her side. He screamed her name as he fell to her knees, pulling her into his lap as he tried to feel for her pulse. Reaching into his pocket, he pulled out his cell phone and called an ambulance.

He couldn't find a pulse. He didn't think she was breathing. He didn't know what happened. She seemed really scared and was screaming, biting on her hand and crying and then the collapse.

The ambulance was on its way.

Her face was sodden, mouth matching her fist in a mix of saliva and blood, snot from her nose and tears from her eyes blended with the film sheen of sweat covering her skin. He was baffled, confused, and frightened. The operator was trying to tell him how to do CPR, but he couldn't get the image of her staring at him like he was a stranger, like he was going to hurt her, out of his head.

The ambulance came. They used the emergency access code to enter the locked door. A large man in the police uniform pulled him back as two blue clad medics began working on his wife. He saw the brief glance they shared, the tightening of the mouths. She was dead.

"What happened?" He barely recognized his own voice.

"Sir, we would like you to tell us." Officer Mark Gallows, or so his name tag stated, looked straight into his eyes. "Perhaps we could attend to your child while I get a statement from you?"

He led the officer out of the bedroom and across the hall. The toddler was standing in his crib, grabbing the rails in his tiny fists as he hiccuped through tears. Reaching down, he picked up his son and hugged him close. The world seemed so small and empty.

"How about we go into the kitchen?"

He nodded and followed the officer out and down to the white tiled room. He automatically went to work making a warm bottle for the baby as the officer took a seat at the bar.

"So what happened tonight?"

"I'm not really sure. She was in the bathroom for a while and I went to check on her. She sounded off but said she was just feeling sick and maybe it was something she ate. We all ate the same thing though. After a bit longer, I was starting to get worried and tried to check on her again. She kept wanting me to go away and was crying and even screaming sometimes. The door was locked and she wouldn't open it. I started to get really scared and as she got more frantic I panicked and kicked the door in. And....and she just stared at me in horror. She was terrified. I didn't know what to do. Then she went all rigid and sort of fell over and I called 911."

"Is there any history of domestic abuse?"

"What?! No. Never." His look of shock seemed convincing to the officer, who nodded and moved on.

"What about psychological issues with Jennifer? Does she have depression or psychotic episodes?"

"No. Nothing like that. She's been so happy since the baby came along. She's writing a book and loves staying home with him. She's always smiling and seems to be glowing. If there was, she hid it so well." He shook his head, staring at the little boy in his arms. Tears flowed freely down his cheeks.

Officer Gallows watched the man. He used his wife's name in the present tense, suggesting he hadn't processed her death and making it less likely he was responsible. He was concerned the man was going into shock. Turning to the side, he radioed for a second medical team. If anything, the man and baby should be checked to make sure it wasn't something environmental.

"Is there anyone I can call for you, sir?" Officer Gallows glanced at the man who had stopped rocking his son back and forth and stood staring at the little boy.

"Sir? Are you okay?" The officer stood and walked around the bar, his hands poised to grab the baby out of the man's arms if something suddenly happened.

Commotion from the hall caused the officer to turn and watch as the medics rolled the covered body toward the front door. When he turned back around, the kitchen was empty.

"Officer Gallows. Dispatch confirming need of a secondary medic vehicle. Is there information on the patients?"

"Um," He turned a circle in the room and stepped back toward the hall, the acrid odor that had struck him when he came in was stronger. "The patient's husband and child."

"Repeat that please."

"The husband and child of the original patient. Just for a check-up and to watch the husband for potential shock."

"Sir, I believe you may be mistaken."

Officer Gallows walked back down the hall. For the first time, he noticed the soot stains on the ceiling. The smell of burned garbage and wet charcoal grew stronger.

"The patient is en route to the hospital. It's suggested you and whoever is remaining at the scene exit the building due to structural compromise from last week's fire damage."

His mouth dropped open as he stared into the baby's room. The paint on the walls was bubbled and black, the floor and ceilings were black. The crib was but a skeleton of ebony. The smell of the burned debris was nearly unbearable.

Officer Gallows spun on his heels and went into the master bedroom. The room was a mess. Items of clothing were everywhere. Minor fire damage around the door frame was nothing compared to the water damage from the fire hoses. The bathroom was a mess. Everything charred, burnt, broken and destroyed.

Back in the hall, he walked down the blackened carpets, glancing into the shell of a kitchen. Absently he rubbed the butt of his pants, not surprised to see the smears of ash when he looked at his hand. The wall behind the stove, the wall that was shared with the nursery, was open, with the blackened studs the only barrier.

"What happened to the husband and child?" Gallows spoke into his radio, his voice wavering.

"They died in a fire last week. It's believed the patient may have had some involvement. She's been missing since then."

Walking blindly, Officer Gallows exited the house. He refused to look back as he walked to his car. Once inside, he pulled out his cell phone and looked up the address. A picture of the man and the toddler was shown with an article about the fire and their deaths. It was believed the woman had looped the gas lines from the stove back into the wall and ignited the fuel. She hadn't let the fumes build up enough or the house would have been in much worse condition.

Looking into the police report, he discovered the man had still been alive, breathing in the black smoke as the fire burned him and the child. The window's electronic fail safe had been turned off and the bedroom door locked. Marks on the other side of the door suggested the man had tried to kick it down. Jennifer Copen was considered a dangerous psychiatric patient who had left the hospital against doctor's orders after her husband admitted her with postpartum depression. There was a warrant for her arrest in connection with the fire.

Officer Matthew Gallows stared at the phone in his hands a while before finally lifting his head to look at the house. A man holding a child waved at him from the door. They were barely recognizable. The skin was black in the places it still hung onto the bones. Their eyes seemed too big and bright. Teeth poked out of the shriveled mouths as they stretched into grotesque grins. The man held up his hand, bones poking out a vibrant white against the charred flesh as he gave a salute.

The officer slowly raised his hand in return. He pushed the button to begin the ignition sequence on the car. He entered the address for the nearest mental health check-up clinic and laid back as the car began its short journey. He wasn't sure if he even dared to close his eyes.

Are you awake?

0800 The shrill beeping of the watch was not nearly as loud as it sounded to me. It used to only sound like the purring of a cat. Not anymore. Nothing soothing about the noise now. It woke me up with a jolt of fear and adrenaline. This is not a welcome to the world of awake, not anymore. No one is welcome anymore.

0830

This is nutrition. I must remind myself it is. It tastes of nothing, thick and sticky, catching in my throat and barely washed down by the meager sips of water. It will give me the strength to keep going. Or so I keep thinking it does. Something does. If it didn't, then I wouldn't be trying anymore. Something is pushing me.

0900

I wonder if the disgust is permanently etched on my face in folds and wrinkles. A heavy brow, narrowed eyes, lips tight and jaw clenched. It doesn't even hurt anymore, the clenching. It should, but maybe that's just how my mouth thinks it should be now.

1000

I know they see me. They see my face. Do they recognize me? I don't. I don't remember who I am. What I am. Something is there, deep down within me. Maybe that's what is pushing me forward. Maybe. I don't know. They don't look for long. Their eyes stray away. Scanning nothing and everything but seeing what is not there. Not anymore. Nothing is there. How can they allow themselves to follow the herd, conform to the false colors and lines? Why don't they look around like me? Really look around and see what isn't there anymore. The food is mush. The sounds are dull. There is no color. There is no smell other than the smell of death. Their faces hang limp, their eyes glassy and far away. They see without seeing.

1130

What's different today? Something is different. A thickness in the air, a hum buzzing around them and me. But it irritates me. They don't seem irritated. In fact, I think I saw one smiling. Smiling! Who does that anymore? When did they learn to do that? Does their face hurt? I saw another one, the corner of their dry lips slightly pulled up. Something is changing.

1200

A dozen smiles and many more smirks. Their eyes are still empty, but there is a stirring. Are they waking up? I fear that. Then they will see me. They will see my anger and hatred. I can't have them wake up. They can't see me!

1500

I'm out of breath. I had to run back to the safety of my home. The wall was pulled back in place for the first time in months. The false shelving lifted by a lever. They saw me. At least three looked straight at me and saw me. They know I am here still. But why are they coming back? What's happening to them? What will they do to me?

1700

The scraping of feet in the hall was frightening enough, but now I hear a low mumble above the buzzing hum. I think they are trying to talk to each other, with their mouths. I didn't know if they could talk. I thought about shouting at them, but I didn't know if I could talk anymore either. What would it sound like?

1830

I think they left. For now. I don't know if I'll sleep tonight. Probably not. They're waking up. I don't know what will happen. I barely remember how it was before, when I wasn't the only one awake. Back when people smiled and their eyes had light. They could hear and speak and talk and see and be something, someone.

2200

I had been asleep, barely, though. I can't put my guard down anymore and today was so unnerving. I'm afraid to sleep. I think I heard something. Maybe it was a dream....no...there it is again. A loud thump and...a giggle? Is that what that sound is? Like bubbles, glass bubbles breaking against the walls. I sit, frozen in fear and staring at the shelves blocking the only door to the hall. I don't know where they usually go at night, but they haven't been in the halls at night in days, weeks, months...I don't know. There are more than one or two. The shuffling of their steps joins the cackles. I pull my legs up, knees to my chest, and wrap my arms around them, burying my head and trying not to scream. It was quiet for so long and I wanted noise again. But not this. Never this.

2345

They know I'm here. The noise is deafening. I can't even guess at how many are out there. What do they want? What will they do to me? I try to think they only want to see me and talk to me. Maybe they are confused by me or maybe they are happy for me. Maybe they are back. Maybe they are awake, finally. But something in my gut tells me that's not what they want. If they find me, I won't be awake anymore. I'll be dead.

0300

My ears hurt. They ring with the foreign sounds that have been assaulting me. The gun is heavy and cold in my hands. Staring at it, I am surprised at how steady my fingers are as they turn it over. My eyes find the dark center at the end of the barrel. Barely visible in the dim light from a dying candle. I wasted my last candle tonight. But I won't need it anymore. There is a loud thump and a scrape. They are getting in. I feel my face pull in an odd angle. I think I'm smiling. When was the last time I smiled? I squeeze the trigger and feel it tighten before the release.

THE EXPLOSIVE SOUND did not give them pause. They knew it was behind the wall. Without speaking clearly, they worked together to uncover the hole. The faint orange glow from within cast odd shadows on the slumped figure. They poured into the room, crowding around the man. He wasn't awake anymore. Their smiles grew wider. He didn't have to be. They were waking up all by themselves. They were a million parts of one. All the smiles led to the same thought, the same mind, connected somewhere. They moved as a solid mass, closing in on the cooling body. Their smiles grew.

Satisfied that the broken one was gone and the dark void in their collective mind had vanished, they retreated back into the night. They were one now and there were no more awakened ones.

As the mob returned to the streets, the elongated figures in the distance nodded in content. What was left of this species were wired in, no longer conscious of being more than machines for the use of the newcomers. They had a fresh planet and a fresh crop and no one to fight back, this time.

Under the Bright Lights

The razor scraped across her skin, catching each hair and snipping it at the root. Kat rinsed the blade and made another pass before moving over an inch and repeating the motion. She hated hair on her legs more than she hated shaving, but she still loathed the necessary process. The razor would apply the same treatment under her arms, across her Mound of Venus, and any other areas where the offending dark specks liked to pop up. She checked the mirror that hung from the back wall of the shower, making sure her lip didn't look fuzzy. Tweezers would take care of the strays between her eyebrows once she was out of the spray of the shower.

After drying off and attacking her face with the tweezers, eyeliner, mascara, and a light lip stain, she felt a bit better. The puffiness under her eyes had gone down, although the bags were still dark. Ignoring the imperfections, she spritzed the body spray in the air and stepped into the falling cloud of fragrance, a process she would repeat once dressed. Bra on, skip the panties, thigh high stockings, short black skirt, and a tight corseted blouse of dark forest green. Her long dark hair was dry enough to push a comb through a few times. She slid her feet into the black leather boots, pulling the zipper up its length to the top of her calf. The black lace choker had a small silver pentacle dangling from the center. Her earrings were onyx tear drops. Three rings on three fingers. One last twirl in front of the full length mirror on the back of her door and she was ready to go.

Kat grabbed her ankle length black coat and purse from beside the door as she headed to her car. She had debated driving herself or having her roommate drop her off somewhere. It had been a long time since she went out and tried to enjoy herself. Knowing she would need to be sober to drive home was a solid excuse not to drink every shot and red plastic cup handed to her. She also didn't want to call her roommate up needing a ride at two in the morning either.

Her unwillingness and inability to make close friends always made these scenes awkward and the general thought seemed to be to just offer her a drink. Kat wondered if they did that because of their own discomfort or because they hoped she would get shitfaced and act as dumb as the majority of the party goers. Why was she doing this to herself again? Loneliness was the easiest excuse and the most accurate, though she never intended on making friends or bringing anyone home.

As she navigated the dimly lit streets, her mind never ceased to pour out one concern after another. She tried to look immaculate so she wouldn't fret about how she looked or smelled or any of that. And yet her brain would find a dozen other anxieties in every corner of the room. She physically shook her shoulders. She was beautiful and smart. Guys would ogle her, girls would envy her, and she would flit amongst the crowd eating up the attention before he got overwhelmed and sent her back to hiding away at home for another few weeks.

The reverberations of the bass could be heard from the small grass lot used as a makeshift parking area. Parking, she pulled in a deep breath, tossed her keys and phone into her shoulder bag and headed toward the metal side door. No signs illuminated the exterior. In fact, only a single streetlight chased back a handful of shadows away from the entrance. The red brick had faded to pinks and oranges over the years. She couldn't remember what the old two-story building had originally been used for but it had spent the last decade as an unofficial party den to their small town.

The door slammed open as she approached, causing her to momentarily freeze in place as two laughing girls, wearing a lot less clothing between them than Kat's entire outfit, stumbled past.

SHADOWS THROUGH THE FOG

Without her coat, she would be freezing, but apparently these two had drunk more than enough to require protection from the chilly night. They barely glanced at her as they headed toward the dark field of haphazardly parked cars. Forcing her breathing to steady, Kat walked through the door, pulling it shut behind her with a barely discernible clang.

The music was deafening and the smell overwhelming. Sweat and the miasmic cloud of various overly applied fragrances caused her stomach to turn. Colors were muffled in the dim, multi-hued lights and flashing strobes. She didn't think drugs would be unnecessary for hallucinations in such an environment. Pushing through the throng of writhing bodies, she aimed for the general direction that the bar had been in the last time she had dared to adventure into the club, if she could call it that. No one really called it by any one name.

It had been at least a year or more sense she had last gone put, much less to the sex and inebriation driven hole that she was in now. Back then she was getting to know her now ex. Now here she was trying to get over the same ex by diving back into the insanity that had put them together in the first place. A small part of her wondered if she was trying to see if he was here or if she was hoping history would repeat itself. Another part was just tired of feeling hurt and empty and was willing to fill the void with whatever took the bait; the bait being her own scantily clad body.

After much shoving, eye rolling, and wedging between the masses, the bar appeared before her. The wooden ledge had long since lost its polish, probably before it was even scavenged for this hell hole. Stained, pitted, covered in gravity, but still solid, the bar stood as a moored boat keeping above the tide of people. A tall, bald man stood behind, tattooed arms crossed over the off-white wife-beater tank top. His eyes were half lidded, as if he was only finely attuned to drink requests and zoning out for everything else. A petite, green-haired girl in a t-shirt cut above her midriff and missing a large portion of the collar, bounced back and forth handing out dripping bottles and cans of beer from the coolers along the back wall.

Kat's eyes scanned the plywood sign on the back wall. The menu of local beers bought at the warehouse outside of town was listed in impressive spray painted lettering. She glanced between the man and the girl. The girl was further away but seemed to be more willing to help, but the man was right in front of her.

"Can I get an Angry Orchard?" She winced internally at yelling the request.

Surprisingly, the man unfolded from his post against the wall, walked to one of the coolers, and opened the bottle for her as he approached her place at the bar. She held out a five, hoping the extra two dollars would win her some favor later in the night. He nodded wordlessly before completing the exchange and returning to the wall to prop himself back up.

Kat sipped from the cool bottle. As the night wore on, the beers would get warmer. They never bothered to refill the coolers with ice. At least they never did before. The tart hard cider was refreshing. Her coat had begun to feel stifling as the heat from all the people boiled around her. She continued to maneuver around the crowd, following the wall to the wood steps that led to a loft above the main floor. They used to have tables and chairs up there, and she hoped that was still true.

Her eyes bounced across the crowd as she ascended. Some faces were vaguely familiar. A girl she may have gone to school with. A guy that offered to buy her a drink ages ago. A chic that was known for making a scene at every bar around in the past five years. None of them were comforting, though, other than knowing that many things stay the same, no matter how much they change.

She paused when she looked back toward the top of the stairs. There were two small tables near the banisters with two chairs each, but a wall stood behind them. A red door was directly in front of the landing. Frowning, she finished the climb and moved toward the door. The handle was some kind of steel. A deadbolt was above the handle. Without thinking, she grabbed the knob and twisted. The knob wasn't locked, but the deadbolt was engaged, holding the door fast. Stepping back, she eyed the door again before looking back out over the crowd. Random faces were watching her, nearly a dozen total, about ten percent of the crowd, and the bald bartender. Their faces were neutral, but their eyes were locked in place as they stood perfectly still. A chill ran down her spine causing her to pull her coat closer, hugging he beer against her chest.

Watching the crowd, she eased toward one of the chairs and sat, placing the beer on the table. The eyes slowly went back to their immediate surroundings, with random glances back in her direction. Kat sipped her beer, feeling unnerved and confused. She tried to remember who had looked at her, which wasn't too difficult when they took turns catching another glimpse at random intervals. She tried to see what the similarities were. Was it some secret club thing? Drugs? Sex? Gambling? None of those would have been particularly surprising. This town was small, but the rural stretches around it had a decent populace, even if they were spread out. Small, farming towns were often secretive about their vices.

There was something, though, that each of the people seemed to share. They were all males, bald, and seemed completely disinterested in what was happening around them. Those that danced were doing so mechanically, not looking at their partner or matching rhythms. The only time their eyes were wide open was when they were looking at her. They didn't look unhealthy, in fact, every single one of them were quite fit and even attractive. She doubted drugs were the secret. Gambling, maybe, but their clothing spoke of middle to low class and there wasn't much to be gambled with when no one had much in the first place. Sex seemed the most plausible. But what? Sex trafficking? Online videos? Her curiosity was consuming her, distracting her from the original reason for being here in the first place.

Taking another sip of her beer, she realized it was already beginning to warm up. She was nursing it and sitting above everyone, alone. It was no surprise when a man headed toward the stairs, his glance bouncing between her, the steps in front of his drunken footfalls, and the group of buddies nodding and motioning from the crowd. Kat rolled her eyes, hoping to catch his gaze and shoo him away. He kept coming. At the halfway point, the red door opened. A bald man stepped out, dressed similarly to all the others, and stared at the drunk. He froze a moment before spinning on his heel, nearly toppling over, and hurrying back down the stairs. His buddies had all turned their backs, looking away from the scene.

"You, come." The man's voice was thick, an accent she couldn't quite place with so few words. He didn't look angry or dangerous, in fact his face was completely neutral, except when he looked back toward the crowd. His jaw would tighten momentarily. Anger? Disgust?

"I....who are you?"

"It is safe. No worries. You are safe. Come on," He met her eyes, a soft smile seemed foreign on his lips, "please."

Kat's brain screamed as she stood and walked toward the open door. She could die. She could be raped. What in the hell was she doing? Of course, wasn't this what she was looking for? She wasn't outright suicidal, but she didn't care much about life lately. Danger. She wanted her adrenaline pumping and her heart racing. She wanted to feel something. And whatever was beyond that door had her heart nearly bursting.

The man stood to the side. She paused watching his face for something, anything that would warn her, convince her, that this was a bad idea. The soft smile returned and he nodded gently.

"You are safe, I promise this."

Russian. It was a Russian accent. She nodded and walked through the door and wondered if she would ever go back out it again.

SHADOWS THROUGH THE FOG

The hall was unremarkable, with the exception of there being only a wooden floor and white walls and a white ceiling interrupted occasionally by simple square fluorescent lights. Not something she would have expected into the top of an old party barn. She couldn't remember how big the loft had been before, but it seemed much bigger now. The hall followed where the right wall would have been, so whatever was to the left took up the majority of the space. But was it one room? Several? Was there another exit? What the hell was going on up here?

The man stopped in front of the only door, white as the walls and on the left. His knuckles wrapped a quick and rhythmic pattern before he reached for the silvery knob. Kat felt herself trembling as she followed him into the dark room beyond. Her mind raced faster than ever, mostly with regret and second thoughts. She was going to die. They were going to rape her. She was so stupid.

Everything seemed to slow as the door was shut behind her. She barely noticed the bald man joining three others and the fact that despite different clothing, they all looked almost identical. In the center of the room was a seating area. The only lighting was a dim chandelier draped in thin, darkly colored fabrics. A long couch sat opposite of her, a love seat to either side. The fabric was an inky black, seeming to consist of nothingness and no material she had ever seen before. An oval, glass table sat in the middle. Brightly colored fish swam in the neon blue depths under the table top, amongst seaweed and coral.

A man lounged on the sofa to the right. Clothed in black, long sleeves and buttons done to half-way up his chest showing a V of dark, tanned skin. Hair the color of dark chocolate fell in loose waves around his angular face and across his shoulders. His eyes were hooded, as if he was dozing or high. His face held no expression. In the center of the large couch was a woman and the focus of Kat's attention. She was beautiful, more than beautiful even. Golden strands of silk cascaded around her ethereal face and down past her waist. She too wore black, a gown that hugged her curves, splitting above her belly button and shooting up to each shoulder, allowing her breasts to tease from each side, smooth and a creamy white. A large red jewel hung between them from a silvery chain. Her bow shaped lips, painted a matte dark red, smiled as her crystal blue eyes locked onto Kat's eyes.

"Welcome, Katara. I am so glad to have you join us." She, too, spoke with a heavy Russian accent. "How fortuitous that you venture here on this night, when I happen to be in the area. I have eagerly awaited our meeting."

Why were there sexy Russian people in this backwoods town? Kat was so confused.

"How do you know me?" She shifted in place, unsure of what to do and afraid to look away from the gaze of the woman. Something in her stomach stirred. She was not unused to attraction to women, but nothing like this.

"I am afraid we do not know each other, not in the normal ways. I know of you and so I have waited to see you. This night was one of decisions. I do not think we will be returning here for quite some time."

Kat shook her head slightly, a thousand questions and her emotions swinging in every direction. Impatience at a straight answer was growing.

"Please, I apologize. Have a seat?" Her hand lifted from her lap, turning over, palm up, in an elegant gesture to the empty love seat.

Having no clue what to expect or what she should do, Kat carefully walked to the sofa. Hands appeared at either side of her neck, causing her heart to stutter, until they grabbed the edges of her coat and gently pulled it away. She felt exposed in her short skirt and tight blouse. Sighing as quietly as she could, she sat on the strange fabric. It felt like fur, but wasn't thick and long like fur. It seemed like suede under her hands, but her eyes couldn't match the texture to the visual. Swallowing her nerves, she slid back until she was leaning against the cushion. It seemed to embrace her from behind. What was this?

"You are frightened. I feel as if I must apologize more, but you do not realize how unlike me these apologizes are. You see," The woman leaned forward, picking up a crystal decanter from the table and pouring the dark red liquid into the three glass chalices around the table. "I am not a humble person. Nor I am I an apologetic person. The truth is I am neither sorry nor troubled. I expected you here and here you are."

The man sat up, grabbing his glass and toasting the air between them before sitting back and sipping his drink. His eyes were so dark, brown or even black. They appraised Kat, scanning her. She shifted, leaning forward to accept the glass the woman held out to her. Her hesitation was ended by the cock of a golden brow. Sipping the wine, her mouth filled with the flavors of dark cherry, chocolate, and something deeper. Nutty, and heavy but completely complementary to the bouquet.

"Delicious?" The man's voice broke her thoughts.

"Ah, yes. Thank you."

"It is one of my favorites. We brought it with us. The beverages here are deplorable."

"What is this about? I am so confused." Kat blurted out as she glanced between the two of them.

"We are here to change your life forever." The woman spoke simply before sipping from her own glass. "Is that not what I am supposed to say?"

Kat frowned into her glass as she took another long drink. There seemed to be an odd bitter flavor creeping in.

"You like?" The man's smile stretched across his face, seeming to be a bit too large, oddly distorted. She blinked, glancing back at the woman.

"Is there something wrong with it? Perhaps you are drinking it too fast." The woman's face showed no emotion, though her eyes were glued to Kat.

The taste clung to the back of her throat. The woman's hair seemed to twist and jerk, like inverted seaweed around her head. Her eyes glittered, almost obnoxiously. Sparkle and flash, the light above growing brighter as she tried focusing on the woman's face.

"It seems she has rushed her drink, Flynn." Her voice was muffling, getting harder to understand as if the accent was turning into cotton in her mouth.

"Tarja, I believe she has done more than that." Both of their mouths curved into Cheshire grins, pulling like taffy and creeping up their cheeks.

"Did...you...drugz...drank.." She watched the glass leave her hand, one of the two she seemed to have no control over. It tipped away and then the base was sliding through her fingers.

There was a clunk as the heavy crystal hit the wooden floorboards. No one moved. But who was there other than the two serpents that lay across the dark abyss on either side of her. Fur nesting below their glittering heads, velvet draped along their slithering bodies. They moved to the central point between them, coming together and then crossing. Their bodies slid out of the fabric as they twined together, twisting into a knotted pile of golden and copper scales. The beaded black eyes of one and the blinding pearls of the other. Was it blind? The lighter one? The eyes seemed to have a pearlescent sheen, like tiny opals caught amongst the ridged angles of its face.

"Ssshheee isssss sssslleeeeping..." the whispers swirled around her head as it floated downward, too heavy to stay atop her high shoulders.

The thunk as she hit the floor, the feel of the wooden grains pressing into her cheek. The wine was thick on the board in front of her. She stuck out her tongue, but it wouldn't reach. It looked like blood.

SHADOWS THROUGH THE FOG

"Sssshhhheeee's done it now. Sssssilly girl. Sssssoooo sssaaddd."

The whispers were gritty, like sandpaper in her ears. It wasn't Russian anymore, or French, or anything. Snakes don't talk. She tried to giggle. Her chest bubbled, but the noise that escaped her mouth sounded more like a gargle and grunt. Her lips were sticky. Her tongue was getting too big for her teeth.

"Oh no. Oh god..." A tickle, from outside of the room. She heard them, banging around. Someone was yelling.

Maybe she peed herself. But the water at her waist was so cold. Everything was cold. Her lips were cold too. She tried to move but the floor held her tight. The icy, slick surface seemed to bond with her skin. When did she shut her eyes? They were so heavy. Maybe her eyes were lead. She tried to laugh and there wasn't even a noise this time.

The banging was louder, more people must have come in the room. She should warn them about the snakes. They might trip and fall on the floor with her. Something warm and rubbery pulled at her eyelids. A bright light pierced through her head. She tried screaming, jerking away, but she still couldn't move. The wine was made of glue. Had to be. Something ripped her off of the floor, breaking the ice crystals that had grown in place and laying her on the soft couch. But it wasn't as soft as it was before.

Something hard crashed across her mouth and nose and a blizzard was poured into her nose. It was a snow globe, or half of a snow globe. How did they cut it in half without spilling the snow on the floor? It was bright behind her eyelids and then it wasn't.

Screams rose and fell in the distance as the ground rushed around her. The grinding of a giant wheel churned below her head. It seemed like forever, and then it faded out.

She was blinded again. Kat wanted to scream at the white swords of light cutting into her eyes. They weren't lead after all. Or they were. Maybe someone had gotten a torch, they could help her keep them open. Everything was cold. The world was cold. The sharp sounds of metal on metal, the cold rubber fingers pulling at her face and arms. Something was pressed into her chest, sticky tentacles, they grabbed and held fast along her abdomen. Where were her clothes?

The air grew thin, she was tired of breathing and tired of seeing the light. The light hurt. Why was she so cold with such a hot light burning into her face and brain? Her mouth moved, she tried to tell them to turn it off. She wasn't sure if her lips worked anymore. And then the light dimmed. As it faded, so did the pain. Although a sound rang in the distance, a loud monotone note. And then it too faded away.

The nurse shook her head as the doctor called the time. They knew it had been a far shot. The roommate wasn't sure how long the girl had been bleeding out in the shower or how many pills she had taken before she used the razor on herself. But it had been enough for her to do what she had set out to do. She was gone from this world.

"She was so pretty. I wish I knew what hurt her so badly to make her do this." The nurse's heavily accented voice was met with looks of sorrow and defeat. She felt her eyes stinging under the bright lights of the operating room. Blinking back the tears, she shook her blonde head and exited the room.

Couch Co-Op

"We're out of smokes." Jay chunked the empty pack at the trash can. It missed and joined its brethren of disposable packaging amongst the floor.

"Hold on." Cole leaned forward, his finger moving across the plastic buttons of the controller.

Jay flopped back on the sagging couch, his eyes following the characters as they bounced back and forth on the screen.

"It's not like you're playing anyone, with the damn servers down. Just pause it. You smoked the last one, like, an hour ago."

Cole moved his hand in a flurry of motion, his hero stood proud, arms in the air over his fallen opponent.

"Yeah, well, now we can play the other levels." The unlocked messages popped up on the bottom of the screen. "Worth it!"

He dropped the controller into his seat as he stood, scrambling around for his wallet and keys.

"You need a car."

"And you need money. That's why we play so well together." Jay blinked his eyes in mock flirtation.

Cole shook his head and they headed to the beat up little compact car. He wasn't fond of driving anywhere, but Jay always had the funds and bought the smokes and cokes, and that carried weight. Cole slumped into the driver seat, mentally bracing for the traffic they could come across. He would never lower himself to voice his concerns, but his anxiety with driving was bordering on being a serious problem. He hadn't driven further than five miles away in several months.

Two stop signs and one major highway crossing, and they pulled into the empty parking lot of the small convenience store. Cole frowned as he looked through the front window.

"Lights are on."

"It's the middle of the day, they're open."

"But where is everyone? Isn't it gettin'-off time for the 9-5ers?"

"Dunno. Maybe there was a wreck or something."

Cole shrugged.

"Get enough so we don't have to come back tonight."

Jay was already shutting the door, and waved back in acknowledgment.

No one could be seen behind the counter. No cars drove by on the busy highway. Cole shifted in his seat. He didn't like people and traffic, but he also didn't like it when it was too quiet. He wondered about the weather. It had a propensity to bring random tornado weather. Maybe he missed an alert on his phone when he was playing.

He watched as Jay walked out of the store, turning back to look through the glass doors before jogging over to the car.

"Dude, no one is in there. The lights are on, cash registers on, but no one's around."

"Did you make sure the guy wasn't sprawled out behind the counter. He could have had a heart attack."

"No, should I?"

Sighing, Cole climbed out of the car and followed Jay back in. There was no old man dead behind the counter, no one in the bathroom, and the tiny cleaning closet was empty. But the lights and register were on and the doors unlocked.

Cole grabbed a small pad of memos and jotted down the cost of two packs of cigarettes and the brand, asked Jay for the cash, and tucked it under the cash register with the corner sticking out.

"I'm not waiting around."

"Should we call the cops?"

"Like I said, I'm not waiting around." Cole grabbed the two packs of cigarettes and headed back to the car.

Jay soon followed after, his head swiveling around as if SWAT was going to rush from the woods and tackle them to the ground for not waiting on a cashier. The whole thing screwed with his head.

"Dude, does this not freak you out? Like, what the fuck?" Jay felt nauseous.

"I dunno. Could be a holiday. That new guy they hired probably went around back to smoke a J or something. Who knows?"

Cole pulled back into the yard and they climbed out, heading inside. As Cole flopped back into his perfectly indented hole on the couch, Jay stood in the doorway, staring around the neighborhood.

"You gonna play or not?"

Jay slunk back inside and dropped to the couch, grabbing one of the packs of smokes and ripping off the plastic.

"Sure."

"Servers are still down. And I'm signed out! What the hell?" Cole jumped up and went over to the router. "No lights. Not red or anything, just nothing."

"Internet's down?"

"I guess. Damn it." Shrugging, Cole went back to his seat and grabbed the controller. "I have two Indie games downloaded, couch co-op. I guess we can do that until everything's back up."

Jay lit his smoke, grabbed the other controller, and sighed.

"I guess. Something seems weird though."

Cole started up the goofy looking side-scrolling beat 'em up. They ran through for almost an hour until they stopped so they could check the internet.

"Still nothing." Cole pulled out his phone. "And no cell service. I do have a message..."

"Who?"

"I dunno. Don't recognize the number."

Jay looked over as Cole's voice faded out.

"Some asshole trolling me. Probably someone I used to know."

He tossed his phone on the cluttered coffee table amidst the empty cans, cigarette butts, and garbage. Jay leaned forward.

Game over. Uninstall.

"Ooookay...."

"Yeah, whatever. We can probably beat this today."

They settled back into the game but Jay had a hard time focusing.

"Are we just doing the same thing over and over?"

"It's an Indie....and a beat'em up, it doesn't change a lot."

Jay wanted to agree but the screen only showed the main menu. And yet he and Cole both were moving their hands on the controller. His brow furrowed in confusion. As he reached for the cigarette pack, he noticed it was empty, but they had only smoked two a piece.

"Where are the other smokes?"

"We need to go get some. You smoked the last one, like an hour ago."

Cole moved his hand in a flurry of motion, his hero stood proud, arms in the air over his fallen opponent.

"Yeah, well, now we can play the other levels." The unlocked messages popped up on the bottom of the screen. "Worth...." He turned to look at Jay. "Didn't we already do this?"

Jay nodded. He stared at the screen and realized it was back to Cole fighting the computer again. He was holding the controller, mashing the buttons. The hero did a final move, arms went up, an unlock message popped up. The room seemed to spin...no, not spin, glitch. The table was clipping through the floor. The back wall of the room seemed to be rendering still, trying to come into focus instead of being a pixelated swath of grays.

"What the fuck?"

And then it all went black. Except for the screen on the television. A blue box popped up.

SHADOWS THROUGH THE FOG

AI character integration has failed. Couch co-op is no longer available. Uninstall and then reinstall "stoner dudes" AI for full re-integration for the VR unit.

The screen flicked off.

Jason groaned, dropping the controller on the floor.

"Man, what bullshit. What's the point of a cool mod if it crashes the game?"

"Dude, it was cool and all, but playing us playing a game is just too meta for me. Whatever. Just load the game and keep the AI thingie off, that shit was depressing."

The Little Lost Faery

Silent as a darkened sky, thinking always why, till she knows that she will cry,
   the little lost faery.
   Wondering so much, far from another's touch, hating the situation such,
   the little lost faery.
   Sing does she not, as the tree below her rots, feeling fear always a lot,
   the little lost faery.
   Never the dragon does she see, for his snack she will be, not a bit of time has she,
   the little lost faery.
   Wide is a gaping hole, in she goes like a mole, for a life has it stole,
   the very big dragon.

Amanda Leanne
January 2004

Don't miss out!

Visit the website below and you can sign up to receive emails whenever Amanda Leanne publishes a new book. There's no charge and no obligation.

https://books2read.com/r/B-A-ERBF-TWUP

BOOKS 2 READ

Connecting independent readers to independent writers.

Also by Amanda Leanne

Shadows Through the Fog
The Fine Print of Fibro
Sever the Circle
Mind the Mirrors

Watch for more at https://amandaleanne.com/.

About the Author

Amanda Leanne began reading at a very young age and has been writing since grade school. She is a prolific reader, book collector, and writer with an interest in all aspects of art including sewing, painting, sculpting, jewelry design, soapmaking, and various other hobbies. After spending nearly a decade working on her degrees in forensic sciences, abnormal behavioral science, and neurological psychology with the prospect of joining the FBI ViCAP unit, Amanda's health took a turn for the worse. Daily struggles with her medical issues hasn't stopped her from pursuing her childhood aspirations to become an author. She currently lives with her spouse (Kris), her son, and their cats in the mountains of Northern Alabama. Leanne writes non-fiction as well as fictional novels. Her non-fiction books and articles delve into topics such as medical conditions, true crime, psychology, and crafting. Her fictional stories delve into horror, psychological, mystery, thrillers, eerie tales, science fiction, and paranormal worlds.

Read more at https://amandaleanne.com/.

www.ingramcontent.com/pod-product-compliance
Ingram Content Group UK Ltd.
Pitfield, Milton Keynes, MK11 3LW, UK
UKHW042004230426
12048UKWH00009B/534